D1362768

Sch

SHADES SHORTS

CRIME

stories

David Belbin
Alan Durant
Gillian Philip
Anne Rooney

Evans

Published by Evans Brothers Limited
2A Portman Mansions
Chiltern St
London W1U 6NR

Shades Shorts: Crime Stories © Evans Brothers Limited 2009
Rockface copyright © Gillian Philip 2009
SMS Murder copyright © Alan Durant 2009
An Open and Shut Case copyright © Anne Rooney 2009
In a Hot Place copyright © David Belbin 2009

First published in 2009

British Library Cataloguing in Publication Data
 Crime stories. - (Shades shorts)
  1. Detective and mystery stories, English 2. Young adult
 fiction, English
 823'.0872080914[J]

  ISBN-13: 9780237536183

Editor: Julia Moffatt
Designer: Rob Walster

Contents

Rockface

Rockface

by Gillian Philip

Lee squinted up at the granite cliff. The sun was dazzling in a blue sky: what a day for climbing. If climbing was what turned you on.

It wasn't where Uncle Frank got his thrills, though Lee could make out his form, high against the rockface, abseiling lower and then scrambling nimbly from ledge to ledge. No, the climb was just a side issue for

Uncle Frank. He got a kick out of it, of course. But not half as much of a kick as he got from the eggs.

Lee checked the video camera was running properly, easing it a little to the left so it stayed focused on the spidery figure. Uncle Frank liked to be centre stage. He'd expect to watch this film over and over again, so Lee had better get it right.

No, he'd better not let Uncle Frank get out of shot, since the man also got a kick out of giving Lee a good kicking. If he really was his uncle, Lee would mind more about that. But he wasn't. It was just that Lee had refused to call him 'Dad', so after some argument and a bit of thumping, they'd compromised on 'Uncle'.

Lee raised the powerful binoculars, searching the sky. The male falcon was there: so high in the cloudless blue he was barely a dot. As he swooped and wheeled lower, though, Lee could tell he was agitated. The female was still on the nest, crouched defensively over her eggs, but as Lee watched she took flight, panicked by the approaching climber.

Lee adjusted the focus, checking Uncle Frank's rope. It was bright red and clearly visible, strained across the craggy rock from the weight of him abseiling down. It had never broken, though.

Uncle Frank was careful with his ropes. He'd ordered Lee to throw one out just the other day, because it had begun to fray. Uncle Frank knew his business.

It was a business only in the loosest sense. Lee might not mind these weekend trips so much if Uncle Frank made any money out of them. Or rather, any money that he passed on to Lee and his mother.

He always seemed to have enough for himself but he'd go ape if Lee's mother tentatively asked for a bigger household contribution. In fact, after the slapping she got last time, she'd stopped asking.

The egg-collecting was for himself, said Uncle Frank. He was an *enthusiast*. It was a hobby, a *passion*. He wasn't in it for the *money*.

Lee had his own theories about that.

The female peregrine was harrying Uncle Frank now, diving at him with frantic, high-pitched cries, and the male was doing the same. It didn't bother the egg hunter. He pressed against the rock, protecting his face, ignoring the birds, and inched closer to the little ledge of rock where they'd scraped out their nest.

Delicately Lee adjusted the binoculars. Yes, there was definitely a new clutch.

Uncle Frank had expected the female to lay again, and sure enough she'd done it. *Most obliging!* cackled Uncle Frank.

Lee had shot him a filthy look, so Uncle Frank had given him a hard clout on the ear that brought tears to his eyes. Lee didn't let them fall, though. He didn't cry any more. It wasn't worth it. It never did his mother any good, when she was cowering under Frank's fists and feet, so Lee certainly wasn't going to give him any more satisfaction.

Sighing, growing bored, Lee adjusted the focus again and peered carefully at the rope. It looked safe enough. Uncle Frank edged down, sideways, closer to the nest.

It seemed greedy to Lee. Unfair, really. Uncle Frank had got the last four, after all: he'd even let Lee take a look at them after he'd blown out their contents and settled them carefully in their new cotton wool nest. The eggs were undeniably pretty. Pale reddish brown, mottled with delicate darker patches.

Still, why did Uncle Frank need the next clutch too? Poor old bird, she'd never lay again this season. Lee reckoned the furtive phone calls were something to do with it. And the texts that followed the calls, the texts that made Uncle Frank's eyes light up with little pound signs.

Not in it for the money, eh? Hah!

There was no point calling the authorities. Uncle Frank would only get a few months inside, like last time. And if it was Lee that put him behind bars, he'd kill him when he got out. Lee shivered. He felt sorry for the falcons, but he had himself and his mother to think about.

Pity, really.

Bored, Lee checked the camera again.

Fine. Perfect. He'd like to stretch his legs, but he didn't dare. Besides, he'd had his exercise already: the long walk across the moor from the car park to the top of the cliff, where he'd fixed the rope while Uncle Frank sorted out his harness and got ready to climb. Watching him as he lowered himself over the edge. Then a check of the rope, an adjustment or two. And finally, the quick unnerving scramble down through the heather and scree of the hillside, and round to the foot of the cliff, just to get a good shot with the camera.

That was half the point, after all. Uncle Frank liked to relive his exploits.

He was like James Bond, he said proudly. Everything was planned to the last detail. He'd worked out the exact best way down the rockface and along to the ledge. He'd done it before. It'd be even easier this time.

Sure enough, he was almost directly above the nest now. The falcons were just about demented. Abseil just a little lower, and he'd be able to reach out and get the eggs. Just like last time.

Once more Uncle Frank pushed himself away from the rock and eased himself downwards, all his weight on the harness.

Poor old birds. Lee found he couldn't watch. He raised the binoculars to the top of the cliff, where the red rope strained across the granite edge. You'd think by now—

The rope snapped.

Lee gasped. The shock was like an electric charge in his body. The tension went out of the rope so suddenly it seemed to hang in the air for a second, vibrating. Then, like an elegant snake, it rippled down the rock.

Lee swallowed hard. He almost didn't

dare look at Uncle Frank, but he managed to focus the binoculars again.

The man hadn't fallen. The rope dangled uselessly from his harness, the end of it just touching the ground. One gloved hand gripped a little outcrop of granite, and he swung by that, grabbing for a second handhold. Lee's breath stuck in his throat.

Come on, come on!

'LEE!' yelled Uncle Frank.

Yes. If he ran fast, and climbed faster, he could take the end of the rope and get to the top of the rockface again and secure the rope somehow. Course he could. That would be the obvious thing to do.

But Lee stood, mesmerised. Shoving one hand into his pocket, he nervously fingered his penknife, then gripped the binoculars with both hands again.

'LEE! Ya stupid wee—' Uncle Frank's

fingertips scrabbled at the second handhold, his legs still swinging. He almost had a grip now. Lee held his breath.

The female peregrine came out of nowhere, like a sickle of steel. Maybe her wingtip actually slashed across Uncle Frank's face: it was hard for Lee to tell, even with the powerful binoculars.

She must have got close enough, though. Uncle Frank gave a shriek, flailing at her, and lost both his handholds.

'It's a bit of a tragedy,' said the ranger to the police constable. 'Egg thief or not, you wouldn't wish an end like that on anybody.'

'And terrible for the lad.' The constable watched the boy being driven away. 'What a thing to witness.'

'They'll go easy on him, won't they?'

'I reckon. Doesn't sound like he wanted

to be involved in the first place. And I shouldn't think he'll follow in his stepfather's footsteps, do you? Not when the footsteps end there.'

He nodded at the foot of the cliff.

'Yuck,' said the ranger, shuddering. 'At least he fell before he got the eggs.'

'All on camera, too. What a thing for the boy to film. Terrible accident.'

'Surprises me, mind you. The man was a repeat offender, big time. We've had trouble with him before.' The ranger shook his head. 'You'd think he'd be more careful with his equipment.'

'Overconfident. Cocky. It happens.'

'Yes, and I saw the broken end of the rope. Very badly frayed. Can't imagine why he was still using it, but I did hear Frank Martin was a cheapskate as well as being a thief.'

'He should have thrown that rope out ages ago.' The constable shrugged and sighed. 'Ah, well. He has no one to blame but himself.'

SMS
Murder

SMS Murder

by Alan Durant

It started with a text. Tom Davies was
sitting on a train on the way to his
girlfriend Laura's house when his phone
vibrated. He thought it would be a text
from Laura chiding him for being late, but
the number of the sender wasn't on his
contact list and wasn't one he recognised.
The message itself turned his easy smile
to a bewildered frown. *Subject dispatched*.

Head for cash mon eve old card.

He stared at the screen. Read the text again. Shook his head. *Weird or what?* he thought. He searched in his mind for possible meanings in the text that might be relevant to him. Could the sender be someone from college perhaps? *Subject dispatched.* What did that mean? And as for the second bit, well, that sounded like some cryptic crossword clue. No, he decided. It had to be a wrong number. The text wasn't meant for him at all. He pressed reply, thumbed in, *Sorry, mate. U got wrong no*, and pressed send. He went to delete the original message, then changed his mind. He'd save it to show Laura. It'd make her smile, which might be useful if she were annoyed with him for being late.

'You could've texted,' Laura reproached him when he finally arrived. But she wasn't really that put out. They didn't have anything planned, just an evening in, watching TV.

'Talking of texts,' he said, when they were sitting down in the front room drinking tea, 'take a look at this. It came out of the blue when I was on the train here.'

He got the text on screen, passed her his phone. She read the message, then looked at him with an expression of amused bemusement.

'Bizarre,' she uttered.

'Yeah,' he agreed. 'I texted back to say he'd got the wrong number.' He laughed. 'Makes you wonder, though, doesn't it?'

'Yeah.' She laughed too. 'Intriguing.'

They spent some time happily speculating what the text might mean:

a message from a recruitment agency for headteachers perhaps or, more fancifully, a taxidermist who'd stuffed a family pet but wanted extra for the head. The last bit of the message was the trickiest to explain. 'Mon eve' was obviously Monday evening, but 'old card'?

'You dispatch cards, don't you?' said Tom. 'Don't get the old bit, though.'

'No,' Laura said thoughtfully. 'Unless it's the name of a place – The Old Card. A pub perhaps?'

'Funny name for a pub,' Tom protested.

'Pubs have funny names,' Laura persisted. 'The Pig and Ferret, The Jolly Duck, The Leg of Mutton.'

'Well, you could have a point,' Tom conceded.

They turned on the TV after that and didn't talk about the text any more.

They were in the middle of watching a mystery movie when Tom's phone rang. He glanced at the display, then frowned: it was the same number as the earlier text.

'Hello,' he answered uncertainly.

'Good evening,' said a deep, confident man's voice. 'I believe you may have received a text from this number earlier today.'

'Yeah,' Tom replied. 'I sent you a reply to say you'd got the wrong number.'

'Ah. The thing is Mr—'

'Davies. Tom Davies.'

'Good evening, Mr Davies,' the man said warmly. 'My name is Russell Smith. I work for a telephone network monitoring company. We've had several complaints lately of texts going to the wrong numbers and we sent out some exploratory texts to see if there was a problem. I wonder, could you confirm for me please the message you received?'

'Sure,' said Tom. He reeled off the message.

'Ah, I see,' the man muttered sombrely. 'It seems there is a problem. You shouldn't have received that text.' There was a slight pause. 'I'm really sorry about this, Mr Davies. It looks like it's a local fault. Could you confirm for me your postcode, please?'

'Well...' Tom hesitated.

'It's just that I can't get rid of the fault unless I can discover where it is,' the man explained. 'I hope you understand. It'll be a nuisance for you if these random messages keep coming through to your phone.'

'Yeah, I guess so,' Tom accepted. He gave the man his postcode. 'My girlfriend and I had some fun, though, trying to decipher the message you sent – especially that bit about the old card.'

'Old card?' the man queried, then laughed. 'Oh that. It was just nonsense, dreamt up by some geek in the office.'

'Nothing to do with headmasters or taxidermists then?'

'I'm afraid not,' the man said, amused. 'Anyway, thanks very much for your time, Mr Davies. You've been very helpful. We'd like to send you a gift for all the inconvenience caused.'

'It was nothing,' said Tom. 'Really.'

'No, it wasn't nothing,' the man insisted. 'I can assure you it wasn't nothing.'

Then he rang off.

'Curiouser and curiouser,' said Laura archly.

Tom shrugged and they went back to watching the movie.

The next day, Tom was at home heating up some soup for lunch, when he got a call from Laura.

'Switch on the TV,' she instructed. 'The news on BBC One.'

'Eh? What, now?'

'Yes, right now.' The urgency of her tone made Tom move with unusual haste. He switched on the TV, tuned it to BBC One. There were shots of police putting up yellow tape round a crime scene.

'The headless corpse was discovered here on the common by a man out walking his dog early this morning. As yet, the dead man has not been identified and police say that they have no idea why or by whom this gruesome murder was committed. Any member of the public with information relevant to this enquiry is urged to call the police task force.'

A number appeared on the screen.

'See?' Laura's voice almost shrieked down the phone.

'See what?' Tom questioned.

'That's the meaning of the text you got: subject dispatched. It's a kind of code, you know, for someone's been murdered. And then "head for cash". The killer's going to hand over the head to whoever hired him to do the murder when he gets his money. It's obvious!' Laura's voice was high-pitched and breathless.

Tom took a moment before responding, hoping this might have a calming effect.

'Laura, you're letting your imagination run away with you,' he said with amused dismissal. 'The text was from a telephone network company. It was a mistake. I had a long conversation with the guy last night, remember?'

'He was lying,' Laura insisted. 'He was

trying to find out about you.'

'This is crazy,' Tom uttered.

'Is it?' said Laura. 'Phone that number back then. Ask for that guy...'

'Russell Smith.'

'Yeah.'

'Ok, I will,' Tom shrugged.

The doorbell rang.

'Hold on a moment, Laura. Just got to answer the door.'

'No!' cried Laura. 'Don't answer it. It might be him!'

'Don't be silly, Laura,' Tom said firmly. He'd had enough of this. Sometimes Laura's imagination was just too wild.

The doorbell rang again. Tom went to the front door and opened it. A postman was there with a package – an ordinary postman holding an ordinary package.

'Thanks,' said Tom taking the delivery.

'See,' he said into the phone. 'I haven't been murdered. It was only the postman.'

He started to unwrap the package. 'It's probably that free gift that guy promised me.' He pulled off the brown paper and found himself holding a small white cardboard box. He lifted the lid, pulled aside the tissue paper— He gasped, withdrew his hands so that the box dropped to the floor, spilling its contents.

'Tom! Tom!' yelled Laura. 'What is it? What's happened?'

Tom stared, horrified, at the gift he'd been sent.

'It's – it's...' he stammered, struggling to comprehend what he was seeing. 'He's sent me – an ear.' His phone vibrated. He pressed to open the text and read the message with horrified eyes: *I'm listening. No blabbing, mate. The Dispatcher.*

Forensic tests confirmed that the ear probably did come from the headless corpse. The police praised Tom and Laura's bravery and public-spiritedness in speaking to them and not bowing to the murderer's threats. They tried the number of the text that Tom had received but weren't surprised to be told that the number was no longer in use or, when they investigated further, to discover that the phone was registered to someone who didn't exist. Russell Smith, The Dispatcher, was a phantom.

'He'll be long gone by now,' a police inspector told Tom and Laura regretfully. 'Out of the country probably.'

To Tom and Laura this news was cause for relief, certainly not regret.

The head was found eventually out at Denham Fort, the old base, as it was popularly known. It was Laura who worked that out. She tapped the message Tom had been sent into her phone, using predictive text. The last word came up as 'base'. She scrolled through the options and, sure enough, card was one of them. It must have been the first on the killer's phone. She was right, then, when she'd suggested that first evening 'old card' might be a place. The head belonged to a known drug dealer, who'd been trying to muscle in on another, much bigger, dealer's patch. No one was charged with the murder; the police reckoned the murderer was a contract killer – not a local man – and the trail soon went cold.

A couple of months later, Tom was on the train to Laura's when his phone vibrated. It was a new phone with a new number (the police had kept the old one as evidence). He had a text. He looked at the number. It wasn't in his contact list, and he didn't think he recognised it, yet— He took a deep breath, steadied himself, went to options, scrolled down and pressed delete. Then he sent Laura a text to order the takeaway. He could murder a curry.

An Open
and
Shut Case

An Open and Shut Case

by Anne Rooney

'This case is closed,' said Inspector Bayliss. 'There is nothing to find out. You've been wasting police time again, young man. That's the only crime here. Don't call about this again – or any other crime you've imagined.'

The policeman handed his empty teacup to Farooq's mum.

'Thank you, Mrs Akbar. I won't take up any more of your time. And I don't expect

you to take up any more of mine,' he said,
frowning at Farooq.

As the door closed, Farooq flopped on
the sofa.

'Idiot,' he mumbled.

'I'm sure he knows his job,' Mrs Akbar
said. Her lips made a tight, thin line.

Farooq wasn't so sure. A policeman
who knew his job would see that using
a chainsaw indoors was a bit odd. He
would think a man dragging a heavy
suitcase to his bin, leaving dark stains on
the ground, was maybe hiding something.
A policeman who knew his job would
follow a lead like that.

'Well, have *you* seen Mrs Armitage?'
grunted Farooq.

'Amanda has gone away. Mr Armitage
said so. Poor man. He's so upset about her
leaving him. It really doesn't help, you

sending the police round.'

'He killed her and cut her up. I know he did. It's so obvious. He put her in the suitcase. Then he dumped her in his wheelie bin.'

'Farooq, you watch too many of those far-fetched movies,' his mother said. She went back to the kitchen, but carried on talking. 'Your imagination runs away with you. The police say he was cutting up wood to make a floor in his loft. He showed them the wood and the saw. It had no blood on it. Only sawdust. There's no law against cutting up wood, even at night. He threw out her clothes and books. And the foods that only she liked. The liquid must have been from them. Don't jump to conclusions, Farooq, it only brings trouble.'

Farooq stared at the television. It was turned off.

'I'm off out,' he said. He slammed the door as he left.

Outside, the street was quiet. Mr Armitage's house was opposite. It was quiet, too. *Quiet as the grave*, Farooq thought. But there was a face at the window. Mr Armitage was staring at him. He looked angry. He'd never liked Farooq. *So what?* Farooq thought. *I don't want to be liked by a murderer.*

He kicked a can along the path. So. The police had asked Mr Armitage questions. They had been to the dump. They hadn't found a suitcase with a dead body in it, cut into pieces. They had found one suitcase that Mr Armitage said was his. It had been mashed up by the rubbish lorry. He said he'd put his wife's books and clothes in it. Why had he thrown them away? Because she had left him for another man, and said

she was never coming back. Where had
she gone?

'Who cares?' Mr Armitage had shrugged.

No evidence, Inspector Bayliss said. No
evidence of wrong-doing, no evidence of
murder, and no body. But Farooq knew.
He just *knew* Mrs Armitage hadn't run
away. She was too scared to leave. He'd
seen her in the garden with her friend, Mrs
Martin, just before Mrs Martin went on
holiday last week.

'He'd kill me if he knew, or if I left him.
He would really kill me. He's a cruel, hard
man,' Mrs Armitage had said. And she had
hidden her face in her hands while Mrs
Martin patted her shoulder helplessly.

Farooq looked over Mr Armitage's fence.
If she wasn't cut up in a suitcase, perhaps
she was buried in the garden. He could
hardly dig up the garden in broad daylight.

But he could dig it up at night.

Farooq went to bed in his clothes. He got up at one o'clock. He opened the back door. Everywhere was quiet. It was raining a bit. He shivered. Then he went to the shed and took the spade. In a few minutes, he was in Mr Armitage's garden. Farooq peered at the muddy ground. He wished he had brought a torch. He couldn't see anything.

That wasn't quite true. He could see a bit. He could see a light through the bushes, in the house. Had Mr Armitage heard him? Farooq held his breath. No one came out. He heaved the spade over his shoulder. Then he moved towards the house as quietly as he could. The rain made a noise on the leaves. When he got closer, he could hear another noise, too. Sawing. Mr Armitage was sawing something up in his kitchen. This time he wasn't using a

chainsaw – he was using a handsaw.
Farooq listened: saw; pause; saw; pause;
saw; pause. He was making hard work of it.
But it wasn't a body. It sounded like wood.

Farooq crept close to the window. It
was dark outside and light inside. If Mr
Armitage looked out, he would see his own
reflection on the window. Mr Armitage was
sawing up planks. He had cut six pieces
already. Maybe they were shelves. But why
cut shelves in the middle of the night? The
ends were splintered and broken. It was old
wood, with bits of paint on it. They
wouldn't be nice shelves.

Farooq stepped back to think. He didn't
want to go home and call the police again.
He knew what Inspector Bayliss would say.
It's not a crime to cut up wood. Wasting
police time.

Mr Armitage put the saw down. He

picked up four planks and left the kitchen. Farooq moved closer. Mr Armitage went through the hall and up the stairs. Farooq saw the landing light go on upstairs. A moment later, Mr Armitage reappeared in the kitchen. He picked up the other two planks. Then he picked up a hammer and went back upstairs. Farooq tried the back door. It was locked. That was a good thing, he thought. Otherwise he would have gone in. Who knows what would happen then? Maybe Mr Armitage would attack him.

Then Farooq heard another noise. Sobbing. Very, very quietly, someone was crying. The noise came from above. He only heard it for a moment. Then Mr Armitage began hammering furiously. He was much quicker at hammering than at sawing. Farooq couldn't hear the crying any more, just the hammering. And he heard his own blood pulsing in his head. He couldn't separate the sounds. His heart was going as fast as Mr Armitage's hammer. When Farooq tried to think, his brain wouldn't work. Should he try to get in the house? Call the police? Go home?

He took a deep breath. If Mrs Armitage was crying she wasn't dead and buried in the garden or cut up at the dump. What was Mr Armitage doing to her with a hammer and some planks?

The police had searched Mr Armitage's house. The house was the same as his own. There were two bedrooms upstairs, and a bathroom. One bedroom was at the front of the house. She couldn't be in there. He wouldn't hear her from the garden. One bedroom faced the back of the house. So did the bathroom. Farooq stepped back into the garden and looked up. Enough light came from the landing to show a dark shadow in the back bedroom. A very tall shadow. Like a person on a ladder. In the back bedroom, there was a hatch to the attic. *The attic*! That's where she must be! And Mr Armitage was nailing wood over the hatch. She was still alive. He was trapping her in the attic, like a prison. Or a living tomb.

There were two things he could do. He could call the police. Or he could break into the house. He was in the garden with a spade. How hard could it be? Farooq hurled the spade through the glass of the door. It made more noise than he expected. The hammering stopped. Mr Armitage came downstairs. He was carrying the hammer. He held it up high. Farooq saw him come into the kitchen and look at the spade. He thought Mr Armitage would come for him. And now he didn't have the spade. He ducked down out of sight. But Mr Armitage didn't come; he just stood there.

All was silent for a moment. Then Farooq heard the sobbing again, ever so quietly.

'Shut up!' muttered Mr Armitage. 'Shut the hell up.'

Farooq took his phone out of his pocket. He dialled the police. He waited till they answered. 'I need help here,' he said. '14 Willesden Gardens.' He ended the call immediately. Surely they would come? He keyed a text message into the phone, but didn't send it. He laid the phone on the floor by the back door. Then he hid in the bushes and waited. Five minutes passed. Ten minutes. Then he heard a car pull up at the front of the house. The police hammered on the front door. Mr Armitage didn't answer. A policeman came round to the garden with a bright torch. He shone it at the windows, then the door. The broken glass sparkled. The officer used his radio to call his companion from the front of the house. As Farooq watched, he trod on the phone. Farooq and the policeman both heard the case crack.

' 'Ere, Gavin,' he said as the second officer arrived. He shone the torch on the phone. 'Look at this. And this.' He flashed the torch at the broken glass. Gavin picked up the phone, using a cloth to save any fingerprints. He pressed a button.

'*She's in the attic,*' he read. 'OK. Radio the station, tell them we're going in.'

Farooq slipped backwards through the bushes and home.

From his bedroom window, he watched another police car arrive, and then the ambulance. The sirens woke his mother.

'What's happening?' she asked Farooq.

'The police are taking him away,' smiled Farooq.

At lunchtime, Inspector Bayliss came to the door.

'I'd like a word with Farooq, Mrs Akbar,' he said.

Farooq followed the policeman into the living room.

'Take a look at this, young man,' he said, handing Farooq the early edition of the evening paper.

There was a large picture of Mrs Armitage. Her face was strained and she was wrapped in a blanket, just as Farooq had seen her getting into the ambulance.

'RESCUED FROM HELL-HOLE,' the headline said.

After a week hidden in an empty water tank, Amanda Armitage was freed by police. 'There's no doubt about her husband's guilt,' commented police spokesman, Roy Bayliss. 'It's an open and shut case.'

'I believe this is your phone,' said Inspector Bayliss, showing it to Farooq. It was in a plastic bag. Farooq could see it was badly scratched and the plastic was broken. He held out his hand. 'You can't have it back yet, I'm afraid. It's needed as evidence,' he said. 'But, er,' the Inspector coughed awkwardly, 'I think I was a bit hard on you. I'm sorry. You were right all along. You'd make a good policeman. Thanks for your help.'

Farooq smiled. Inspector Bayliss fumbled in the pocket of his police jacket.

'You might need this,' he said, pulling out a box. 'If you'd like to have it. It's a little thank you from me and Mrs Armitage.' The policeman coughed again and handed Farooq the box. It was the latest camera phone, ultra-thin, ultra-slick – the model everyone wanted. 'It does video, too,' Inspect Bayliss went on. 'In case you see something suspicious. Collect some evidence next time, eh?' And he shook Farooq's hand.

In a
Hot Place

In a Hot Place

by David Belbin

They grab you outside the airport. They put
a bag over your head.

'Why are you doing this?' you ask.

But if they can hear, they do not answer.

'Where are my friends?' you ask.

You were with two mates. Your plane
leaves in an hour. Will your friends go
home without you?

They put you in the back of a van.

'Why don't you search me?' you ask. 'I've done nothing wrong. I've been on holiday.'

They don't reply. They take off the bag and put on a blindfold. They put you on a plane.

When you get out of the plane, you are in a hot place.

'Where are we?' you ask.

Nobody answers. They take off the blindfold. It's dark. They put the bag back on your head. You find it hard to breathe. At least they can't see you crying. You are hungry, but you're too proud to complain. Now and then they give you a sip from a water bottle. The water tastes old, bitter. The drinking straw hurts your dry mouth.

They put you in a cell. You do not know if it is day or night. All the time, you hear shouts and screams. You do not understand the words. You begin to shout too.

'I was on holiday! I did nothing wrong!'

Nobody comes.

'I didn't have a bomb!' you protest. 'Why did you take me, not my mates? Or did you take my mates too?'

Days pass. They take off the blindfold. At last, the questions begin.

'Why were you there? What did you do? Who do you know? Why were you there? Who did you see? What did they ask you to do?'

The room used to be white. Now the walls are covered in stains. The stains look like blood, sick, urine and worse. The room smells like a toilet. They tie you to the chair and put plastic cuffs around your wrists.

'What am I doing here?' you ask.

'We ask the questions,' they say.

'I've done nothing wrong,' you say.

'Then you have nothing to worry about,' they say.

'I'm only fifteen,' you say. 'I want my parents.'

'Were your parents with you?'

'No. I was with friends. Are my friends here too?'

'No. Did your parents send you?'

'They paid for my holiday,' you tell them.

You want them to know this was all a mistake. You were on holiday. It was only a holiday. You are not a terrorist. You do not want to be a terrorist. You did not meet any terrorists. You do not want to overthrow anybody. You only want to go home.

'Your parents paid, did they?' they say. 'Then maybe we will bring your parents here too.'

'What am I supposed to have done?'

'You tell us.'

You don't know what to say, so you say, 'No comment.'

This is the wrong answer. More men come. They put the hood back on. They begin to hit you. They hit you on the heels. They hit you on the head. They punch you in the tummy. They are hitting you in places that will not bruise. It hurts so much, you wish they would ask more questions. You beg them to ask more questions.

'I'll tell you anything you want to know,' you say.

But they do not believe you. Their questions are always the same.

'Where did you go? Who do you work for? What did you do? Where did you do it? What do you believe? Who do you plan to kill? Who are you working with?'

'I don't want to kill anybody!' you say.

'We all want to kill someone,' they say.

"Why won't you let me go? I've done nothing.'

'We've all done something,' they say.

'I want a lawyer!'

They laugh.

'You don't have any rights here,' they say.

'Where am I?' you ask.

'Nowhere. Tell us who you work for.'

'I don't work for anyone,' you say.

They do not believe you. They take your clothes off. They tie you to a wooden board. They put a plastic bag around your face. It has a hole in it. They pour water through the hole. You begin to gag.

'I'll tell you anything!' you say.

They take the bag off. You make things up. You tell them what you think they want to hear.

They do not believe you. They tie you to another board. They put the bag back on.

'I did it!' you say. 'Whatever you say I did, I did it!'

A lawyer comes to see you. You tell her what happened. 'You have no bruises,' the lawyer says.

'They are very good at not leaving bruises,' you say.

'It took your parents months to find you,' the lawyer says. 'They thought you were dead. What did you do?'

'I did nothing,' you say.

'That's what everyone says,' the lawyer says. 'But they usually have their reasons. What did you do?'

If you knew the answer, you would tell her. 'Nothing,' you say.

'I'll try to get you out,' the lawyer says.

'Don't I have rights?' you ask.

'Nobody has rights here,' the lawyer says.

She goes away. She does not come back. They leave you in a cell for weeks on end. You speak to no one. But you dream. You have bad dreams. You dream they are right. You really are a terrorist. In your dreams, you understand why people become terrorists. Because you hate people like them.

You are about to turn sixteen, but are not sure when. There are no clocks, no calendar. Then they give you a birthday present. It hurts a lot. You ask to see a doctor. They give you one.

'You seem healthy to me,' the doctor says.

'This is healthy? I can't move my arm.'

'You still have your eyes, and your feet are still at the ends of your legs.'

'Are you really a doctor?' you ask.

They hit you again. They ask more questions. They hurt you again. They ask more questions. They hit you with questions. They ask more hits. They question your hurt. They ask you again. You question their hurt. They hit you.

'You are not one of us,' they tell you.

'I am not one of them,' you tell them.

After a long while, a different lawyer comes.

'You have human rights,' he says.

You do not believe him.

'People are asking questions about you,' he says.

You ask who these people are.

'Your parents would like to visit you,' the lawyer says, 'but they are not allowed to.'

'I don't want them to see me like this,' you say.

'What did you do to make them take you?' the lawyer asks.

'I was on holiday.'

'Why were you on holiday there?' he asks.

'My friends have family there. We stayed with them.'

'Have you or any of your family or

friends ever been in trouble?'

'I don't know. Maybe.'

'That is the wrong answer,' the lawyer says. 'You and everyone you know have to be innocent. If not, it means you're guilty. That's how the system works.'

'How can I be sure of a thing like that?' you say.

'You have to say what I tell you to say,' he says.

So you say what he tells you to say. And you wait. And you wait. And they ask you more questions. But you can tell they're getting bored.

'Are you one of them? Are you one of us?'

You say, 'No.' And you keep saying, 'No.' And, after a long time, they get tired of asking you questions. They even get tired of hitting you. And they stop. And they agree to release you, as long as nobody makes a fuss. So you don't make a fuss. And they let you go.

Your family are very glad to have you home.
Your friends are very glad to see you.
They're very sorry they left you behind. But
your friends have moved on. You're not the
same, and neither are they.

You go to college to make up for what you
missed. You make new friends. You explain
where you were. Some people are impressed.
Some ask you to join the fight. 'You know
who the enemy are. You know what they are
afraid of. Help us to get them,' you are
asked. 'Give them what they deserve.'

'What have you got to lose?' you are asked.
'Do you want them to think they won?'

You are not afraid. You say you will think
about it. You think about it. You think about
it. You're not afraid.

You think about it.